Ariel and the Aquamarine Jewel

by Lara Bergen

Illustrated by Studio Iboix
and Andrea Cagol

DISNEP PRESS

New York

$\mathcal{I}$t was a glorious summer morning—a perfect day, thought Ariel, for a walk along the shore. Happily, she set out, then suddenly stopped when her foot struck something hard in the sand.

"Ouch! My toes!" she cried, still not entirely used to the feel of human feet. She bent down and dug out something shiny in the sand.

"Why, it's a jewel!" Ariel exclaimed. She'd never seen anything like it in the human world before. "Scuttle," she said quickly to her seagull friend, "please go find Sebastian and ask him to fetch my father." Perhaps it had come from the sea! If so, her father might know more.

A short while later, Ariel's father, King Triton, emerged from the waves. "Ariel, my dear!" he declared. "Hello, Father," she said. "I found this lovely jewel. Do you know where it came from?"

King Triton's eyes grew wide. "Why, yes, indeed I do!" he replied. "In fact, I'll *show* you," said the king. Of course, he first had to change Ariel back into a mermaid. And with a blast from his mighty trident, that's exactly what he did.

Gripping the water-colored jewel, Ariel excitedly dove into the sea. But as she entered her father's throne room, her enthusiasm faded.

"Why, it looks like a tidal wave's been through here!" she cried. "And Atlantica's treasure—it's gone!"

"Alas," said King Triton, "it's true. For a thousand years, our treasure chest has kept our kingdom's treasure safe. And then one giant wave comes and washes it all away! That aquamarine is just one of dozens of gems that were lost, I'm afraid."

"Don't worry, Father," said Ariel. "I'll help you find the other jewels! After all, I'm a pretty good treasure hunter, if I do say so myself!"

First, Ariel searched the old sunken ship—a place she still knew like the back of her fin—swimming in and out until she'd found a dozen jewels. Then, she and Flounder went to the coral reef. With a little help from some other friends, they found more lost jewels. And by the time the tide turned, Atlantica's treasure chest was full again!

"Ariel, on behalf of Atlantica, I thank you,"
said King Triton.

"I'm just glad all the jewels are back where they
belong," she replied.

The King thought for a moment. "Actually," he
said, "I'm not sure that they are all where they belong."
And with that, he reached into the treasure chest and
pulled out the first, and by far the most beautiful,
aquamarine that Ariel had found. Then he gave his
daughter a kiss and placed it gently around her neck.

That night, back at her own castle, Ariel told Prince
Eric all about her adventure. As she did, she touched her
precious jewel and gazed out across the sea. Though she
knew that her father was never far away, it still felt good
to have a piece of Atlantica with her, always.

No sooner had Aurora said the word than the Queen took the crown from her head and proudly placed it on Aurora's. (And then, some say, the heart-shaped diamond shone brighter than ever before!)

Aurora hurried back to the castle and up to the sewing room.

"I've solved the riddles!" she said brightly. She took a pink rose from her hair and handed it to her mother. Then Aurora bent down to give the Queen a kiss on her cheek.

"Very good!" declared the Queen. "And the answer to the third riddle?" That's when the fairies flew in with Prince Phillip.

"It's *love*," said Aurora, "of course!"

"Let's see," said Aurora. "It could be a tree. That gets stronger the longer it lives. And I suppose you could say that it's blind. But then so are bats." She thought and thought . . . until at last Prince Phillip arrived.

"Happy birthday, my love!" he called, walking up with his horse, Samson—and almost instantly, Aurora knew the answer to the third riddle.

"Now it's my turn!" exclaimed Merryweather. "Ahem." She cleared her throat.

"What only gets stronger the longer it lives?
What pays you back tenfold the more that you give?
Some say it's blind, some say it's true,
Some just say simply, 'I feel this . . . for you.'"

Merryweather giggled. "Silly me! I almost said the answer!"

"Very good!" exclaimed Fauna. "And now for the second one:

Some plant it, some steal it, some blow it away.
Some do it several times in a day.
Some who are shy might blush getting this
On their hand or their cheek. Can you guess? It's a . . ."

"Well . . ." said Aurora, thinking. "If 'some plant it,' it might be another flower. . . . But what can you get on your 'hand' or your 'cheek'? Oh, I know!" she declared. "It's a kiss!" And she planted a kiss on each of the fairies to prove it.

With that, the Queen told
Aurora to go to the garden. There, the
fairy Flora recited riddle number one:

"To the eyes, it's a treat; to the nose, a delight.
But beware! To the hand it can be quite a fright.
Though few think to taste it, its sweetness still shows.
To this very first riddle, the answer's a . . ."

"Hmm . . ." said Aurora. "'To the eye, it's a treat.' So it's pretty. . . .
'To the nose, a delight.' So it smells good. . . . 'To the hand . . . quite
a fright.' So it must hurt . . . like a thorn on a rose. That's it, isn't it?
A rose!"

Happily, the Queen led
Aurora through the castle
to a great portrait hall.
It was filled with stately
paintings, each of a lovely
young princess wearing a
crown just like the one
the Queen was wearing.

"Why, Mother!" exclaimed
Aurora. "Is that you?"

"Indeed, it is," replied the
Queen. "It was painted on my
seventeenth birthday. It's a
tradition in our kingdom that
on a princess's seventeenth
birthday, this crown be passed
down to her, to be worn until
the day the princess herself
becomes queen. But first,"
her mother went on,
"a princess must answer
three riddles to earn it."

Aurora awoke one sunny morning in the most cheerful of moods. It was her seventeenth birthday, and she could not wait to see what surprises were in store. Just then, her mother, the Queen, came in wearing a crown Aurora had never seen before.

"Mother!" cried Aurora. "What a beautiful crown! Is it new?"

"Actually," replied the Queen, "it's quite old. And it's the reason I've come to you so early on this special day."

Aurora
and the
Diamond
Crown

by Lara Bergen

Illustrated by Studio Iboix
and Gabriella Matta

Disnep PRESS

New York